GREAT ILLUSTRATED CLASSICS

THE WIND IN THE WILLOWS

Kenneth Graham

adapted by
Malvina G. Vogel

Illustrations by
Lorna Tomei

BARONET
B·O·O·K·S

BARONET BOOKS, New York, New York

GREAT ILLUSTRATED CLASSICS

edited by
Joshua E. Hanft

Contents

About the Author

Kenneth Grahame was born in 1859 in Edinburgh, Scotland. His parents died when he was a very young child, and he and his sister and two brothers went to live with their grandmother in Oxford, England. Kenneth attended school there, but the family didn't have enough money for him to go to the university. So, when he finished school, he went to work for the Bank of England.

Writing was a pastime Kenneth Grahame enjoyed, and he wrote several collections of stories about childhood experiences, but these were mainly for adults to read. His major story for children, *The Wind in the Willows*, began as a bedtime story he made up for his four-year-old son Alastair, who was nicknamed "Mouse." It was published as a book in 1908.

The tale of River Bank and its delightful inhabitants brings to life the reality of animal life below and above the English countryside and adds the magic and excitement of the animals' adventures. Grahame brought his four heroes to life by giving them very human dress, very human homes, very human life styles, and especially very human personalities: bold, adventurous Mole; efficient, practical Rat; wise old Badger; and proud, exasperating, incorrigible, reckless Toad!

The Wind in the Willows has become one of the most enjoyable and popular series of adventures to capture the imagination of children everywhere. Its success helped ease some of the unhappiness in Grahame's life before his death in 1932.

Brooms and Dusters and Whitewash

CHAPTER 1

River Bank Friends

Mole had been working very hard all morning doing spring cleaning in his little home beneath a large meadow. He had been working with brooms and dusters and a pail of whitewash. When his aching back and weary arms couldn't lift the whitewash brush one more time, he flung it down and shouted out, "That's it! Hang spring-cleaning!"

He rushed out his little door into the steep tunnel, scratching and scraping with his paws until his snout reached the bright sunlight in the meadow.

The warm breezes and the happy songs of the birds welcomed him as he ran along on all fours. "I'm free!" he cried. "No more work for me! Let the birds work building their nests. Let the flowers work making buds. Not me! It's time for me to have fun!"

Mole's happy wanderings took him to the edge of a gurgling, flowing river, the first he'd ever seen. "What a strange animal this is!" he said. "It grips things and carries them along, only to fling them aside and catch something else, all while it's sparkling and chattering and bubbling."

He ran alongside the river until he had tired himself out. Then he sat down on the bank and listened to the babbling stories the river seemed to be telling him.

"And what's that?" he wondered as he spotted a dark hole just above the water on the opposite side of the river. "It looks like a perfect home for any animal who enjoys peaceful waterfront property!"

"I'm Free!" He Cried.

Soon, something bright and twinkly winked at him from the hole. It was an eye, followed by the rest of the little brown face—small, neat ears, and thick, silky hair and whiskers. It was the Water Rat.

The two animals looked cautiously at each other across the river, then the Water Rat called out, "Hello, Mole! Would you like to come over?"

"How do you expect me to do that? I'm not a water animal, so I don't swim."

Rat chuckled as he untied a rope and pulled on it until a small blue boat appeared from behind some bushes. Since Mole was new to the river, he had no idea what a boat was or what it was used for.

Rat rowed quickly across the river and held up his front paw to Mole, who eagerly stepped in and sat down.

"This is my very first time in a boat!" said Mole happily, as Rat shoved off and began to row again. "It's so nice!"

Something Bright and Twinkly

"It's absolutely the *only* thing to be doing on a day like this! It doesn't matter whether you're going somewhere or nowhere, whether you're doing something or nothing. If you're doing it in a boat, it's the best time ever! Say, if you've got nothing to do for the rest of the day, we could row down the river together."

Mole leaned back against the soft cushions and smiled dreamily. "That sounds wonderful!" he said. "Let's start at once!"

"We will, in just a minute. First, I have to stop at my house," said Rat as he tied the boat up to a little dock and disappeared into his hole.

A moment later, he came out, staggering under the weight of a heavy wicker lunch basket. "Shove it under your feet," he said to Mole as he jumped back into the boat and took up the oars again.

"What's inside?"

"Cold chicken and coldtonguecoldhamcold beefpickledpicklessaladfrenchrollsgingerbeer

12

"A Boat Is the Best Time Ever!"

lemonadesodawater—"

"Stop! Stop!" cried Mole, overjoyed. "This is too much!"

"Do you really think so? It's only what I take on all of my little excursions."

Mole didn't hear a word Rat was saying as he lay back dreamily, trailing his paw in the water.

The Water Rat, being a polite, considerate animal, didn't disturb his guest until Mole sighed blissfully, "Life on the river seems wonderful!"

"It is. The river is my food and drink, it's my company and my world. It gives me fun and excitement, whether it's flooding my basement in winter or drying up into a mud bed in summer."

"But isn't it a bit dull at times with no one here to talk to?"

Rat sighed and smiled. "You're new, of course, so you don't know. River Bank is so crowded nowadays that many of my neighbors

"The River Is My Food and Drink!"

are moving away. But those that are still here are always wanting you to do something with them."

"And what's that?" asked Mole, pointing with his paw to some dark woods off to one side of the river.

"Oh, that's the Wild Wood. We River Bank people don't go there very much."

"Why? Aren't the people there nice?"

"W-e-ll, let me see. The squirrels and the rabbits are all right, but you never know with the weasels. And of course, there's dear old Badger. Nobody bothers him. At least, they'd better not!"

Mole was curious about Badger, but he knew that it was not polite for animals to ask "why." So he pointed off in the distance and asked instead, "And what's that blue and cloudy stuff beyond the Wild Wood?"

"That's the Wide World, and it's of no concern to us. I've never been there and I'm never going, and neither are you if you've got any

"What's That?"

sense. Don't ever talk about it again, please!"

Mole was even more curious, but they had just reached a small lake, and Rat was heading towards the calm, grassy shore.

"We'll stop here for lunch," said Rat as he tied the boat to a branch and helped Mole ashore.

"Please let me carry the lunch basket and unpack it," pleaded Mole.

Rat was only too happy to let his excited guest do the work, and he sprawled out on the grass to rest.

When the tablecloth had been spread and all the food packets opened, Rat sat up and said, "Let's dig in."

Mole was glad to "dig in," since he had been hard at work with his spring cleaning all morning and hadn't stopped to eat.

When both animals' stomachs had been filled, Mole turned his attention once more to the water and to a streak of bubbles traveling along the surface. "What's that?" he asked.

"Let's Dig In."

Rat looked at the trail of bubbles and made a cheerful chirping sound in that direction.

Moments later, the broad, whiskered head of Otter appeared on the surface and headed for the bank. Hauling himself out of the water and shaking his glossy fur coat, Otter called out, "What greedy beggars you are! Why didn't you invite me to your party, Ratty?"

"We didn't plan this," explained Rat. "It was an impromptu lunch. But I'd like you to meet my friend, Mr. Mole."

Otter smiled and held out his webbed paw, which Mole shook. Then Otter went on to explain, "Everyone seems to be out on the river today, so I came here to the lake to get some peace, but even here—"

At that moment, a rustling noise in the hedge behind them turned their attention to the striped head and high shoulders of Badger coming towards them.

"H-mmm! Company!" he grunted, then turned away from them and disappeared from

Otter Appeared on the Surface.

view.

"Don't mind him," explained Rat. "He just hates society. He won't bother us. Now, Mr. Otter, tell us who's the 'everyone' out on the river today."

"Toad, for one, in his brand new boat, wearing brand new clothes and brand new everything!"

The two old friends looked at each other and began to laugh.

Rat explained to Mole, "For a time, Toad was interested only in sailing. Then he tired of that and took up punting, pushing a long pole along the bottom of the pond. Last year, it was houseboats, and he swore that he'd live on one for the rest of his life. We all had to live with him on it and pretend we liked it. He's the same with anything he takes up. He's interested in it for a while, then gets tired of it and goes on to something new."

"But he's such a good fellow, it's hard to refuse him anything," added Otter. "All the

The Two Old Friends Began To Laugh.

same, he's not to be trusted in a boat. He can't seem to keep it right side up!"

Just then, a canoe came into view. The short stout figure paddling seemed to be having a hard time keeping the boat from rolling from side to side. Rat stood up to wave, but the paddler shook his head and kept on rowing as hard as he could.

"That's Toad," explained Otter. "He'll be out of the boat and in the water in a minute if he keeps rolling like—" But before Otter could finish his sentence, a mayfly flitted before him. In one swift movement, Otter snapped it into his mouth and disappeared back into the water, leaving only a streak of bubbles behind him.

Although Mole was curious about Otter's sudden disappearance, he knew it would be impolite to ask "why." So, instead, he offered to pack up the lunch basket.

On the trip back, Mole was beginning to feel quite at home in a boat, but he was getting

A Canoe Came Into View.

restless doing nothing. "Ratty! I want to row," he said. "Please let me!"

Rat smiled and shook his head. "Not yet, my young friend. You need a few lessons. It's not as easy as it looks."

This quieted Mole, but only for a few minutes. His jealousy of Rat's skill in rowing was increasing. "I can do it just as well!" he said to himself, and he jumped up and seized the oars so suddenly that Rat was taken by surprise and fell backwards into the bottom of the boat. Mole took his place on the seat and reached the oars out towards the water.

"Stop it, you silly fool!" cried Rat. "You don't know how to row! You'll turn us over!"

Mole tried to dip his oars into the water, but swung them at the air instead. The force of his swing sent his legs flying above his head, and he soon found himself lying on top of the outstretched Rat. He made a grab for the side of the boat, but the next moment—sloosh! Over went Mole, Rat, and the boat!

Over Went Mole, Rat, and Boat!

The water was ever so cold and ever so wet as it filled Mole's ears on the way down. He coughed and sputtered on the way back up, and was about to sink again when a firm paw gripped him by the back of the neck and an oar was shoved under his arms. Rat was laughing as he dragged Mole to shore and hauled him up on the bank.

"Now, my young friend," said Rat as he wrung some of the wet out of him, "Start running up and down the path until you're warm and dry. I'll dive for the things from the boat and recover the boat as well."

A while later, it was a shame-faced Mole who took his seat in the boat. "Ratty, my generous friend," he began, "I'm really very sorry for my foolish behavior. Can you forgive me and still consider me your friend?"

"That's all right, dear Mole. What's a little water to a Water Rat! I'm in it more than I'm out of it anyway. Don't give it another thought. We'll head for home now, but I *do* think that

He Dragged Mole to Shore.

you should stay at my house for a while. I can teach you to row and swim, and make you as handy on the water as any of us."

"Oh, thank you, Ratty!" exclaimed Mole gratefully as his eyes filled with tears. "You're the best friend I ever had and this is the best day of my life!"

This, then, was the beginning of a wonderful summer. Mole learned to swim and to row. He learned the language of the river as it gurgled past his window and he came to understand the whispers of the wind as it blew through the willows.

"I Can Teach You to Row and Swim."

Sitting on the River Bank

CHAPTER 2

Mr. Toad of Toad Hall

One bright summer morning, Rat was sitting on the river bank, singing a song he had just made up and not paying much attention to Mole, who was chattering beside him.

After he had asked Rat the same question over and over, Mole tried one last time. "Ratty, please take me to meet Mr. Toad. You've talked about him so much that I'm really anxious to meet him."

"Certainly," said Rat, jumping to his feet. "Why didn't you say so? We'll go immediately. Toad is always glad when visitors come and sad when they leave. He's really quite good-natured, even though he's not too clever."

The two animals jumped into the boat. By now, Mole had become an good oarsman, so he began to row. When they reached a bend in the river, a fine-looking brick house came into view. Its well-kept lawns and colorful flower beds reached down to the river.

"That's Toad Hall," said Rat. "It's one of the nicest houses in these parts, though we never admit it to Toad because he's so boastful and conceited. On the right are his stables, and on the left, by the creek, is the boathouse where we'll leave the boat."

"But the sign at the boathouse says 'Private. No Landing Allowed,'" argued Mole.

"Don't pay any mind to it!"

Once they had rowed into the boathouse, Mole looked at all the fine boats hanging from the beams and pulled up on slips. "Why aren't any of them in the water?" he asked.

"When Toad became interested in boating,

A Fine-Looking House Came Into View.

that was all he spent his money on. But I guess he's gotten tired of it and has taken up some new fad to keep busy with. We'll find out soon enough."

Once their boat was tied up, Rat and Mole headed across the lawn. They found Toad relaxing in a garden chair, busy examining a large map spread out across his knees.

Seeing his visitors, Toad jumped up and called, "This is wonderful, Ratty! I see you've brought a friend. I was just about to send a boat for you. I need your help."

"With your rowing, I'd guess," said Rat. "Your oars have been splashing too mu—"

"O, pooh!" interrupted Toad. "I gave up boating *long* ago. It was a waste of time. I've discovered the only really worthwhile occupation to devote my life to. Come with me, dear friends, and I'll show you."

Mr. Toad led them to the coach house. In front of it was a shining red gypsy wagon. "There it is!" he announced. "This little cart

Toad Relaxing in a Garden Chair.

will take me on all sorts of adventures along the open road, into villages and towns and cities. I'll be able to travel the whole world whenever I please. Come inside and see how I furnished it."

As they stepped inside, Toad said proudly, "See how comfortable this is. I've got sleeping bunks, a folding table, a stove, bookshelves, pots and pans, biscuits and lobster and bacon, and cards and dominoes. Everything's here that we'll need for our journey this afternoon."

"Did I hear you say *'we'll'* and *'journey'* and *'this afternoon'*?" asked Rat.

"Now, dear Ratty, don't go getting upset," pleaded Toad. "You've just *got* to come. I couldn't possibly manage without you. You really can't want to stick to your musty old river all your life and only go boating. I'm going to show you the world, my boy!"

"I *am* going to stick to my river *and* go boating, just as I've always done. And Mole is going to do it with me too."

"To Travel the Whole World."

"I'll go along with whatever you say, Rat," said Mole loyally. "But I must admit Toad's adventure *does* sound like fun!"

Toad was watching them both very closely and decided not to push Rat for now. "Let's go into the house and have some lunch," he said. "We don't have to decide now. Really, I was only planning the trip to please you."

While they ate, Toad shrewdly gave his full attention to Mole, painting glorious pictures of the exciting times they could have on the trip. Soon, everyone seemed to be taking the trip for granted, even Rat, who hated to disappoint his friends.

When lunch was over, Toad led his friends to the stable and hitched his old grey horse to the wagon. Then the three friends set off along the road. It was a glorious day and the beginning of a glorious adventure.

They traveled until late that evening, when they stopped to eat dinner on the grass beside the wagon.

Beginning A Glorious Adventure

Once they were in their bunks in the wagon, Toad said sleepily, "This is the real life for a gentleman, not your old river!"

"But I like my life in the river!" argued Rat, "and I think about it all the time."

Mole squeezed Rat's paw and said, "If you're that unhappy, Ratty, I'll go home with you in the morning."

"No, we'll stick it out, but thanks anyway. I have to stay just to be sure Toad is safe. Besides, this is another of his fads, and it won't last very long. They never do!" The following morning, Mole and Rat woke early and took care of the horse and made breakfast.

By the time Toad woke up, everything had been done. "What an easy life this is!" he exclaimed. "No worries! No cares! No housework! No cooking!"

On the second night, the two guests made certain that Toad did *his* share of making dinner, and the following morning, Toad was hauled out of bed to work alongside them.

In Their Bunks

That afternoon, they were walking beside the wagon along a hilly road when from behind them came a strange hum, almost like the buzzing of a faraway bee. Glancing back, they saw a cloud of dust with something dark at the center. The cloud was coming closer at an incredible speed, with the buzz becoming a strange pop-pop noise. Then suddenly, a huge, shiny motorcar appeared.

Rat and Toad jumped off the road as the car sped past them towards the wagon. Mole tried to grab at the horse's reins, but the animal reared, plunging them both into a deep ditch, with the wagon crashing onto its side behind them, wrecked!

Rat rushed back to the road, shaking his fist at the speeding car and shouting, "You villains! You scoundrels! I'll have the law on you!"

Toad, however, sat down in the middle of the road and just stared in fascination at the disappearing motorcar.

Mole managed to quiet the horse, then went

A Huge, Shiny Motorcar Appeared.

to inspect the wagon. What a sorry sight it was! Panels and windows were smashed, axles were bent, a wheel was off, and food was scattered all over the ditch.

Rat joined him, and even with the two of them pushing, there was no way they could right the wagon.

"Hey, Toad!" they called. "Come help us!"

But Toad never answered them. He just sat, still staring, as if in a trance. "Wonderful, glorious sight!" he murmured dreamily. "That's the *real* way to travel, the *only* way to travel! Here today, gone tomorrow! And to think I never *knew*! I never even *dreamt*! Oh, what clouds of dust I'll kick up along the road! Oh, what horrid little wagons I'll fling into ditches! Oh, what—"

"What are we going to do with him?" Mole asked Rat in alarm.

"Nothing!" answered Rat firmly. "I've seen him like this before when he starts on a new craze. He'll be in a happy dream for a few days

What a Sorry Sight It Was!

and useless for anything else. But never mind him now. We've got to see what can be done about the wagon. It can't travel in the shape it's in. We'll have to get to town and send someone back to get it and repair it." And taking the horse's reins, Rat started to walk.

"But what about Toad?" asked Mole. "We can't leave him sitting in the road like that. Suppose another one of those motorcar things comes along?"

"I've had enough of Toad for one day!"

The two friends hadn't gone very far when they heard a pattering of feet behind them. Toad caught up and pushed himself between them. He thrust a paw inside each animal's elbow, but still stared dreamily ahead.

"Now, look here, Toad!" snapped Rat. "As soon as we get to town, you're going right to the police station and make a complaint against the owner of that car. Then you'll go to a blacksmith and have the wagon taken there and repaired. Mole and I will find an inn

"But What About Toad?"

where we can stay until the wagon's fixed and you come to your senses."

"Police station? Complaint?" murmured Toad dreamily. "Why would I *complain* about that beautiful, heavenly car? And *repair* the *wagon*? Heavens, no! I never want to see that wagon or hear of it again! Oh, Ratty, how grateful I am to both of you! If you hadn't come on this trip with me, I never would have seen that glorious machine!"

"He's hopeless!" said Rat. "As soon as we get to town, we'll take a train home."

Seven miles later, they arrived at a town. After leaving Toad at the railroad station and paying a porter to watch him, Mole and Rat arranged for the horse to be taken to Toad Hall and for the wagon to be picked up and repaired.

Eventually, a train came along and took the three to a station near Toad Hall. Toad was still in his trance as Rat and Mole led him home and turned him over to his house-keeper.

"We'll Take A Train."

Then they got into their boat and rowed home.

The following evening, after a day of lazing about on the River Bank, Rat went out to visit some of his friends. When he returned, he brought news for Mole.

"The whole town's talking about Toad today. He went into town on the early train and guess what he ordered? . . . A very large and very expensive shiny new motorcar!"

Then They Rowed Home.

Mole Wanted to Meet Badger.

CHAPTER 3

The Terror of the Wild Wood

For a long time Mole had wanted to meet Badger, who was considered an important person with an influence on everyone around him. Mole often asked Rat to introduce him to Badger, but Rat always put him off, explaining "Badger'll turn up some day when it suits *him*."

"But couldn't we invite him to dinner or something?" asked Mole.

"He wouldn't come. Badger hates society and dinners and all that sort of thing."

"Then couldn't we go to visit *him*?"

55

"That's not a good idea. Badger's very shy and even I, who know him very well, have never done that. Besides, he lives in the Wild Wood."

"Well, what's wrong with the Wild Wood?"

"Nothing, really," said Rat, wanting to end this conversation. "He's not at home this time of the year anyway. Just do as I say and wait till he comes here."

Mole gave up asking, and during the summer that followed he was distracted with the fun he was having with Rat. But when fall came, then winter, he began to think about Badger again and wanting to visit him in his hole in the Wild Wood.

For Rat, winter brought a lot of sleeping, going to bed early and getting up late. During his few hours awake, he would write poems or entertain other animals who dropped in to chat around the fire.

By now, Mole was becoming bored. So, one afternoon, while Rat was dozing in his arm-

Rat Would Entertain Other Animals.

chair, Mole made a decision. "I'll go out by my-self and explore the Wild Wood. Perhaps I'll meet Mr. Badger."

It was a cold, gray afternoon when Mole started across the countryside. All the trees were bare and leafless, but that did nothing to dampen his spirits as he headed towards the darkness of the Wild Wood.

When he first entered the woods, nothing frightened him, not the twigs crackling under his feet, not the logs that tripped him, not the funguses on tree stumps that took on the shapes of strange creatures. To Mole, this was fun. So, he pushed farther on, deeper into the Wild Wood.

Soon, darkness began surrounding him, then little faces began appearing from holes in the ground, only to disappear when he turned for a closer look.

He hurried along, telling himself, "Stop imagining things, you silly Mole, or you'll go—"

But he stopped as hundreds of faces seemed

Mole Started Across the Countryside.

to appear all around him, faces with evil eyes that stared at him with spite. "I'll leave the path and go off into the woods," he decided. "They won't follow me there."

Then the whistling began, first behind him, then up ahead of him, then on either side of him. Mole halted in his tracks. "They're after me, whoever they are, and I'm alone and unarmed and far from help. And it's so dark!"

Then the pattering began. "Is it falling leaves?" he asked himself. "No, it's footsteps." Were they in front of him or behind him? The pat-pat-pat grew and closed in on him from all sides. He stood still, as a rabbit came running towards him through the trees.

"Get out of here, you fool!" muttered the rabbit as he ran past and disappeared down a burrow in the ground. "Get o-u-u-u-t!"

The pattering continued and grew louder all around him. The whole wood seemed to be running hard, chasing or being chased. In a panic, Mole began to run too. He ran aimless-

Evil Eyes Stared At Him.

ly, hitting up against things, falling over things, darting under things.

At last, he stopped, breathless, and hid himself in the hollow of an old beech tree. He was just too tired to run any farther. He snuggled down into the dry leaves which had blown into the hollow and, as he lay there, cold and frightened, panting and trembling, he suddenly realized, "This is what Rat was trying to protect me from—the terror of the Wild Wood!"

"The Terror of the Wild Wood!"

Mole's Cap Was Missing.

CHAPTER 4

Lost in the Storm

Mole had left Rat dozing in his armchair, warm and comfortable near the fire. Suddenly, a log in the fireplace slipped and the flames crackled, waking Rat with a start.

He looked around and called, "Moley, where are you? Moley? Moley?"

But there was no answer. The house seemed strangely quiet.

Rat went out into the hall and noticed that Mole's cap was missing from its usual peg and his galoshes were missing from the floor beside the umbrella stand.

"Where's he gone off to now?" mumbled Rat as he opened the front door and poked his head out. "Why, there are Mole's tracks in the mud, and they're leading straight across towards the Wild Wood! I'd better go after him!"

So, Rat strapped a belt around his waist and shoved two pistols into it. Then he picked up a thick club and hurried out the door.

It was almost dusk when he reached the outer edge of the trees of the Wild Wood, and he entered with no hesitation and no fear. The little faces that popped out of holes vanished immediately at the sight of the brave Rat with his pistols and club. And the pattering and whistling, which had begun when he entered the woods, stopped too.

Rat bravely crossed the Wild Wood on the path, then turned and wandered off into the underbrush, calling all the while, "Moley, Moley, Moley! Where are you?"

After about an hour, a weak voice answered him. Following the sound of the voice, Rat

Mole's Tracks in the Mud.

made his way to the foot of an old beech tree and called once more, "Moley! Moley!"

"Ratty, is that really you?" came a weak voice from inside a hollow in the tree. "I've been so frightened!"

Rat crept inside the hollow and said to his trembling friend, "Moley, you really shouldn't have done this. No one from River Bank comes here, especially not alone and not without the magical passwords and tricks that can get you safely through. But never mind that now. We'd better start for home while there's still some light."

"Dear Ratty," said the poor Mole, "I'm simply too exhausted to move. I must rest a while longer if I'm to have the strength to make my way back home."

"All right," said the kind-hearted Rat. "Take your rest." And while Mole slept, Rat stood guard, with a pistol in each paw.

When Mole awoke a while later, the two friends prepared to leave for home. But a sur-

Rat Stood Guard.

prise greeted them outside the hollow.

"It's snowing and snowing hard," said Rat as they looked out across a gleaming carpet of white covering the ground. "Still, we've got to make a start somehow. The problem is, I don't know exactly where we are."

But the two set off bravely, holding onto each other and pretending to be cheerful as they trudged along. The snow was getting so deep they could barely lift their small legs from one step to the next. And the wind was blowing so hard, they were often pushed back more than they were moving ahead.

After two hours, they stopped and sat on a fallen tree trunk to catch their breath. Their bodies were aching and their clothes were drenched from all the tumbles they had taken. There seemed to be no end to this wood, no way out!

"We can't sit here too long," said Rat. "It's getting too cold and the snow is getting too deep for us to walk though."

The Two Set Off Bravely.

"What can we do?" asked the shivering Mole.

Rat looked around and pointed ahead of them. "See the dell over there, that small valley covered with little rounded hills? Perhaps one of those hills has some sort of cave or hole with a dry floor where we could rest until we both have our strength back. By then, maybe the snow will have stopped."

So they got to their feet and struggled down into the dell. They were investigating one of the hills when Mole suddenly tripped and fell forward on his face.

"Oh, my leg!" he cried, sitting in the snow and holding his leg in his front paws.

"Poor Mole! You're not having much luck today," said Rat kindly. And he got down on his knees to look at his friend's leg. "Yes, Moley, you've cut your shin."

"I must have tripped over a branch or tree stump," sobbed Mole miserably. "It hurts!"

"It's a clean cut," said Rat as he bandaged it

Mole Suddenly Tripped.

with his handkerchief. "But it wasn't made by a branch or stump. It looks more like a cut from the sharp edge of something metal."

Rat got up and began scraping in the snow around them. He scraped and scratched, with all four legs working busily, until he cried out, "Hooray! Come and see, Moley!"

Mole hobbled to where Rat was dancing happily in the snow. "*See?* See what?" demanded Mole. "I'm seeing nothing that I haven't seen lots of times before at everyone's front door. It's a plain and simple door-scraper to clean the mud off our feet. I can't see why you're so happy to see a door-scraper that you'd do a dance when I'm in such pain!"

"But don't you see what it means, you dumb animal?"

"It means some careless and thoughtless person has left his door-scraper in the middle of the Wild Wood where it's sure to trip someone."

"Oh dear!" cried Rat. "You *are* dumb! Just

Rat Was Dancing in the Snow.

stop arguing and come help me scrape." And he began to dig through the snow again.

Soon they uncovered a very shabby doormat, and Rat exclaimed triumphantly, "See, what did I tell you?"

"Absolutely nothing!" snapped Mole in exasperation. "You've found another piece of junk someone has thrown away and you're happy about it. So, go ahead and do your dance again. Why you're so happy, I'll never understand. We can't eat a doormat or sleep under a doormat or sit on a doormat and have it give us a ride home over the snow!"

"Do you mean to say that this doormat doesn't *tell* you anything?"

"Really, Ratty, don't you think you're being foolish? Who ever heard of a doormat *telling* anyone anything?"

"I can't believe how thick-headed you are! Just scrape and dig on the sides of all the hills around us if you want someplace warm and dry to sleep tonight." And Rat began to dig

He Began to Dig Through the Snow Again.

furiously in a snowbank beside him, poking it every few minutes it with his club.

Mole sighed, fearing his friend had lost his senses. But he began digging too, for no other reason than to pacify his friend.

After about ten minutes, Rat's club struck something that sounded hollow. The two animals soon cleared the snow away and uncovered a wooden door. On it was a brass plate neatly engraved with the name: MR. BADGER.

"Rat, you're a wonder!" cried Mole. "You're absolutely brilliant, the way you figured out that a door-scraper and doormat meant we were at someone's door! Oh, Ratty, if only I had your head, I'd—"

"But you haven't! And you're not doing much good sitting in the snow and talking. Get up and start banging at the door with me!"

A Brass Plate Engraved: MR. BADGER

Badger Opened the Door Wide.

CHAPTER 5

Mr. Badger

After what seemed like a very long wait, Rat and Mole heard an angry voice grumble through the door, "Who is it *this* time, disturbing people on a night like this?"

"It's me, Rat, and my friend Mole. Please, Badger, let us in. We've lost our way!"

"Oh, my dear friend Ratty!" exclaimed Badger, opening the door wide. "Come in at once, both of you. Why, you must be frozen and almost dead, being out on such a night!"

By the light of the candle in Badger's hand, the two animals saw their host in his long dressing-gown and ragged slippers. He led them down a long, gloomy passage filled with tunnels and heavy wooden doors.

Stopping at one such door, Badger flung it open and the two animals entered a large, warm, fire-lit kitchen. Two long benches with tall backs faced each other in front of the fire, and two other plain benches were at a long wooden table. An armchair at one end of the table was pushed back and the remains of Badger's interrupted supper were waiting for him.

"Sit here by the fire and warm yourselves," said Badger. "Take off your wet clothes, and I'll bring you dry things."

Badger left the kitchen and returned a few minutes later with dressing-gowns and slippers for his guests. Then he set about fixing a fine meal for them.

Badger sat in his armchair, watching the two animals stuffing their hungry mouths, then listened as they told of their frightful

Badger's Kitchen

adventure. When their tale was done, he asked for news about their part of the world and about his friend, Mr. Toad.

"Foolish Toad's gone from bad to worse," Rat replied. "He had another smash-up last week. He's convinced that he's a great driver and no one can teach him anything."

"How many has he had?" asked Badger.

"Smash-ups or cars? . . . Oh well, it doesn't matter. It's all the same thing with Toad. This is the seventh!"

"He's been in the hospital three times," added Mole, "and he's had to pay huge sums of money in fines."

"That's part of the trouble," explained Rat. "Toad's rich, but he's not a millionaire. With his driving record and his fines, sooner or later he'll be killed or ruined. As his friends, shouldn't we do something?"

"You know, of course, I can't do anything *now*," replied Badger.

Rat and Mole understood. No animal who

He Asked for News.

hibernates is ever expected to do anything during the winter, when it was his time to sleep or rest and stay indoors.

"But when spring comes," continued Badger, "we'll take Toad in hand and bring him back to his senses. And now, my friends, it's time we were all in bed. Don't hurry to get up in the morning. You can have breakfast any time you want."

Badger led his guests to a long room that was half-bedroom and half-storeroom, with piles of apples, turnips, and potatoes, baskets of nuts, and jars of honey. But the two little white beds were all that interested Rat and Mole. They jumped in between the sheets and moments later were sound asleep.

It was very late the next morning when the two animals came into the kitchen. A bright fire was burning and all sorts of breakfast food were laid out on the table. Rat began cutting slices of bacon while Mole dropped eggs into a pan. A note from Badger was propped up on

Two Little White Beds

the table. It read:

The snow is very deep outside and it doesn't look as if you'll be able to get out today. Please eat whatever you wish and make yourselves at home. I'll be busy in my study this morning and do not wish to be disturbed.

Rat and Mole understood what Badger meant by "being busy in his study." It wasn't polite for a host to plead sleepiness when he had guests, so it was simpler to explain his need to sleep as being "busy."

While Rat and Mole were eating, the front doorbell rang. When Rat went to answer it, he was surprised to see Otter.

"I thought I'd find you here," said Otter, as he followed Rat back into the kitchen. "Everyone at River Bank was alarmed that you and Mole never came home last night. We all feared that something terrible had happened, but I knew that any time someone was in trouble, they went to Badger. So I came straight here. Even passed a rabbit on the way

He Was Surprised to See Otter.

and after a few well-placed smacks, I got the truth out of him. He knew that Mole here had been lost and scared in the Wild Wood last night, and he admitted that none of the rabbits even offered to help him. Well, I gave him a few more smacks for that. . . . Say, Mole, how about fixing me some slices of ham while I chat with Ratty? I haven't seen him in ages."

Mole was glad to prepare some breakfast for Otter. It was during Otter's second helping that Badger came into the kitchen, yawning and rubbing his eyes. "It must be lunch time," he said. "Let's all sit down and eat together."

Otter eagerly agreed, always ready for an extra meal. "I sure am famished after my long trip here."

During lunch, Rat and Otter continued their conversation. That left Mole and Badger together. Mole took this opportunity to tell his host how comfortable his home was.

"It's a good feeling, being underground," Mole said. "Nothing can happen to you and

"Let's All Sit Down and Eat Together."

nobody can get to you. Things go on overhead and they don't bother you. When you want to go up and out, you can, and everything's there waiting for you."

"That's exactly the way I feel," said Badger. "The only place there's peace and security is underground. If you want to expand your home, all you need to do is dig and scrape. On the other hand, if you feel your house is too big, you close up a hole or tunnel and there you are. And above all, there's no weather to worry about. If the river rises, Rat has to move out. And even though Toad Hall is a fine house, if there's a fire, Toad's got to get out too. That's not for me. Underground's the *only* place to have a home!"

After lunch, Badger took Mole on a tour of his home. Mole was amazed at its size, and at the furnishings everywhere, amazed that one animal had done it all.

Badger explained, "No, I didn't do this all myself. Once, long ago, there was a great city

Badger Took Mole on a Tour.

here, but the people suddenly left and no one knows why, or where they went. In time, the winds and rains covered the city with sand and soil and seeds. Trees and bushes grew in the sand and soil, and soon after, animals and birds found this place. That's how the Wild Wood came to be."

"I've met some of those animals," said Mole, "and they're not exactly friendly."

"Yes, so you told me. But try to remember that it takes all sorts of creatures to make a world. I'll pass the word around tomorrow that Mole is my friend, and no one will bother you anymore."

When they returned to Badger's kitchen, they found Rat pacing nervously. His over-coat was on, and his pistols were thrust into his belt. "Come along, Mole," he said. "We have to leave while it's still light."

"I'll go along too, to lead you," added Otter. "I know every path blindfolded."

"That won't be necessary," said Badger. "My

Rat Was Pacing Nervously.

tunnels run underground to the very edge of the Wild Wood, though I don't care to have everyone know about them. I'll lead you to one of these shortcuts."

Badger took down his lantern and led his three visitors along a damp, airless tunnel that climbed and dropped through earth and stone for what seemed like miles.

When daylight finally appeared at the end of the passage, Badger said goodbye to his friends. Then he pulled the branches and brush and leaves back over the opening, so that it was as hidden as before.

Once outside, Otter took charge. He led Rat and Mole away from the Wild Wood and back towards the river, towards home and all the things that were familiar to them.

One of the Shortcuts

"The Hour Has Come!" He Announced.

CHAPTER 6

From One Prison to Another

It was spring, and Mole and Rat were looking forward to getting their boat in the water for the summer. They spent their days painting and varnishing, mending paddles, repairing cushions, and doing all the little jobs necessary for getting a boat ready.

One morning, as they were finishing their breakfast and making plans for the day's jobs, they received a surprise visitor. It was Mr. Badger!

"The hour has come!" he announced.

'What hour?" asked the puzzled Rat as he

looked at the clock on his mantlepiece.

"Why, Toad's hour, of course. I said I would take him in hand as soon as winter was over and I'm going to do it today."

Badger sat down in an armchair and told his friends, "I learned just this morning that a powerful new motorcar is being delivered to Toad Hall today. I'm certain that at this very moment, Toad is dressing himself in his ridiculous driving clothes. We must hurry and rescue him before it's too late!"

"Right you are!" cried Rat and Mole.

With Badger leading the way and Rat and Mole following behind in single file, the three animals set off on their mission of mercy.

They didn't stop until they reached the driveway of Toad Hall, where a chauffeur was parking a shiny red motorcar.

The door to the house was suddenly flung open, and out swaggered Mr. Toad, dressed in an enormous overcoat, cap, and goggles. As he was drawing on his long driving gloves, he

Off on Their Mission

caught sight of his friends.

"Hello there, my good fellows!" he called out. "You're just in time to come with me for a jolly—er—jolly—" But the serious looks on his friends' faces interrupted his invitation.

Badger strode up the front steps and told his two friends, "Take him inside."

As the struggling Toad was carried inside, Badger turned to the chauffeur. "I'm afraid Mr. Toad has changed his mind. Please take the car back." Then he joined the others inside the house and shut the door.

"Now then, Toad, take off those ridiculous things!" he ordered.

"I will not!" replied Toad angrily. "What is the meaning of this outrage?"

"Then we'll take them off for you!"

Rat sat on Toad while Mole pulled off his driving clothes bit by bit. Once that was done, the Terror of the Highway was merely Toad again, giggling weakly as he stood up and looked from one friend to the other.

"Take Off Those Ridiculous Things!"

Badger scolded, "You knew this would happen sooner or later, Toad. You've ignored all our warnings. You've continued throwing away all the money your father left you, and you're giving us animals a bad name by your furious driving, your smash-ups, and your battles with the police!"

Then putting his arm around Toad's shoulder, Badger continued gently, "We all know you're a good person at heart, Toad, and I'm going to make one last attempt at reasoning with you. Come into the library and we'll talk in private."

Once the library door had closed behind Badger and Toad, Rat and Mole seated themselves in armchairs and waited. "This will never work," sighed Rat. "*Talking* will never cure Toad. I know him. He'll agree to anything, then go out and do as he pleases."

From the other side of the door came sounds of long, drawn-out speeches by Badger and heavy, anguished sobs from Toad.

Badger Scolded Toad.

After an hour the door opened, and Badger led a limp, sobbing Toad out by the paw. "My friends," he said to Rat and Mole, "I am pleased to tell you that Toad has seen his mistakes. He's truly sorry for his actions and has given me his solemn promise to give up motorcars forever."

"That's very good news," said Rat with some doubt in his voice. "If only—" But a twinkle in Toad's eyes made him stop.

Badger didn't notice this as he went on. "There's only one more thing. Toad is going to repeat his promise in front of you both."

There was a long pause as everyone waited for Toad's promise. But what they heard was "No! I'm *not* sorry for what I did. It was a wonderful, glorious experience, and I'll do it again the first chance I get!"

"I told you so!" muttered Rat.

Badger rose to his feet. "Since you have gone back on your promise, Toad, I'm convinced that words have no effect on you. We'll just have to

"Toad Has Seen His Mistakes."

use force instead."

"You can't force me to do anything!"

"My dear friend," said Badger, smiling slyly, "you have often invited the three of us to come and stay with you at Toad Hall. Well, now we're accepting that invitation. We'll stay here until you come to your senses!" Then he turned to Rat and Mole and said, "Take him upstairs and lock him in his bedroom. Then we'll make our arrangements."

Although Toad kicked and struggled, Rat spoke kindly to him on the way up. "It's for your own good, Toady. Think of all the fun we'll have together once you're over this craziness of yours."

And Mole added, "We'll take care of everything for you and see that your money isn't wasted. Just think, there'll be no more incidents with the police and no more weeks in the hospital!"

When the bedroom door was locked and the three animals had gathered again downstairs,

Toad Kicked and Struggled.

Badger warned them, "We must be on our guard at all times. Toad must never be left alone for an instant. He's so determined to follow this craziness of his, there's no telling what he might do. We'll take turns sleeping in Toad's room at night and divide up the day into shifts."

At first, Toad was very difficult to handle. He would pretend his bedroom chairs were motorcars and drive them wildly around the room. Then depression would overtake him and he would lie in bed, almost lifeless, even though his friends tried to interest him in other things.

One morning, when Rat came on duty to relieve Badger outside Toad's door, Badger told him, "Toad's still in bed, and when Toad's quiet like this, he's up to no good. He can be a sly and convincing actor. Be on your guard!"

Rat approached Toad's bedside and cheerfully asked, "How are you today, old chap? It's a fine morning to jump up and go out. And

Pretending His Chairs Were Cars

boating season is beginning too."

"Dear, kind Rat," murmured Toad weakly, "if only you understood how serious my condition is, how I'll probably never be able to jump up or go boating again. But don't worry about me. I never want to be a burden to my friends. In fact, I probably won't be for much longer."

"Well, if that means you're ready to come to your senses, I'll do anything to help, whether it's a burden or not."

"Thank you, dear Ratty," gasped Toad weakly. "In that case, I must beg you to hurry to the village and bring back the doctor... before it's too late... no, I can't ask that of you. That would be too much trouble. Forget that I asked."

"Look here, old man," said Rat, beginning to get alarmed, "of course I'll go for the doctor. But surely you're not *that* sick! Let's talk about something else."

"Talk won't help me now," whispered Toad sadly. "And while you're in town, please ask

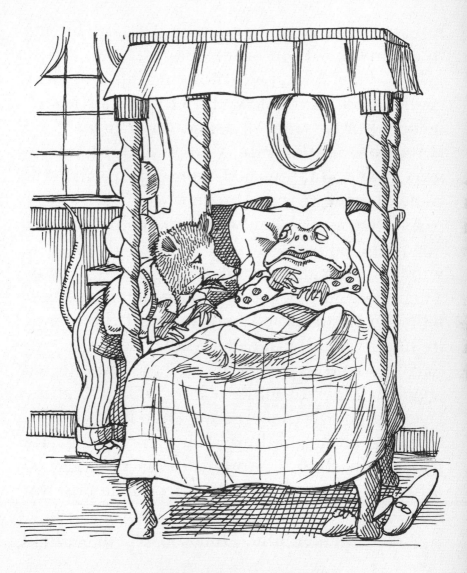

"Bring the Doctor."

my lawyer to come too. I fear it's time for me to get my affairs in order before I—"

"Oh, dear! A lawyer!" thought Rat. "He must really be bad. I've known him to act a little sick before, but he's never asked for a lawyer. I'd better be on the safe side and do what he asks." And Rat hurried from the room, still remembering to lock the door.

As soon as the key was turned in the lock, Toad hopped out of bed and watched from the window as Rat hurried down the driveway. Then, laughing heartily, he dressed in his best suit and filled his pockets with all the money he had in his dresser drawer.

He pulled the sheets off his bed and knotted them together to make a long rope, which he tied to a pole at the window. Then he slid down to the ground, smiling at his cleverness. He began whistling a happy tune as he marched off in the opposite direction from the one Rat had taken.

When Badger and Mole returned to Toad

He Slid Down to the Ground.

Hall, the embarrassed Rat had to face them with the news of Toad's disappearance.

"You, of all animals, Ratty!" scolded Badger. "You, who warned everyone else about Toad, *you* were taken in by him!"

"He was so convincing this time!"

Badger sighed. "The worst part is, now that Toad's gotten away with this, he'll think he's so clever that he'll try to get away with anything and everything. We'd better stay here for a while longer. He may be brought back sooner than we think—on a stretcher or between two policemen!"

Meanwhile, Toad was happily skipping along a high road many miles from Toad Hall. He had taken hidden paths and crossed several fields, often changing direction, just to throw off anyone who might be following him.

"What a smart piece of work on my part!" he told himself. "Brains came out the winner against brute force! Poor old Ratty! He's a good fellow, though not too smart. Perhaps one day,

Happily Skipping Along

I can teach him a thing or two."

With these conceited thoughts filling his head, Toad entered a town. The sign of "The Red Lion" in front of an inn reminded him that he hadn't eaten anything yet that day. So, in he marched and ordered the finest luncheon served in the dining room.

Toad was halfway through his meal when a familiar motorcar sound of pop-pop from out in the street made him drop his fork and tremble with pleasure. The pop-pop got louder, then stopped right outside the inn. Moments later, two men entered the dining room, talking happily about the wonderful motorcar that had brought them there.

Toad listened for a while, then couldn't bear it any longer. He paid his bill and hurried out to the inn yard.

"There can't be any harm in just *looking* at it," he told himself as he slowly walked around the car, inspecting it, admiring it, and touching it lovingly.

He Ordered the Finest Lunch Served.

"I wonder if it *starts* easily."

And the next moment, Toad was turning the handle and listening joyfully to that familiar pop-pop sound. Then, as if in a trance, Toad found himself in the driver's seat, pulling the lever and swinging the car around the yard, out through the archway, and onto the road. In his trance, he had no idea of right or wrong or even what might happen to him.

As he speeded up and headed for the open country, Toad was still in his trance. He knew only that he was Toad the Terror, Toad the Lord of the Trail who had the power to make everyone else get out of his way or be smashed into nothingness!

Toad came out of that trance only when he found himself standing in a courtroom and hearing a judge speaking.

"You have been found guilty on three counts: stealing a valuable motorcar, driving recklessly, and fighting with the local police who tried to arrest you. Because there are *three* crimes,

That Familiar Pop-Pop Sound

not just one, I will impose the stiffest sentence possible: one year for the theft, three years for reckless driving, and fifteen years for what you did to the police officers. That adds up to nineteen years, but I'll round it off to an even twenty! Take him away!"

So, shrieking and praying and protesting, Toad was dragged off in chains from the court-house, across the town square, to a grim old castle whose courtyard was filled with armed guards and snarling dogs.

The police sergeant turned him over to a toothless old jailer with the warning, "Watch out for this vile Toad! He's sly and crafty, and will try to fool you the first chance he gets. Guard him well or you'll pay with your own head!"

The old jailer led the helpless Toad down into a dark dungeon, where the prisoner flung himself on the cold stone floor, sobbing in despair.

"Toad, you're now in the deepest dungeon in

Toad Dragged Off In Chains

the best-guarded castle in all of England!" snarled the jailer. "No one has *ever* escaped from here and no one ever will!"

Then the great door clanged shut and the rusty key turned in the lock.

"This is the end!' sobbed Toad. "Rich, handsome, popular Toad who has been imprisoned unjustly! Everyone who once knew me will forget all about me. Wise Badger! Intelligent Rat! Sensible Mole! What will become of me? Me, unfortunate, unhappy, forsaken Toad?"

"No One Has Ever Escaped from Here!"

She Was Very Fond of Animals.

CHAPTER 7

A Hare-Brained Escape?

In the days and weeks that followed, Toad repeated his cries with no one listening. He refused all his meals and paid no attention to the old jailer's offers to bring in anything the rich Toad might want from the outside . . . for a price!

The jailer had a daughter, a pleasant, good-hearted girl who was very fond of animals and even kept a bird, a squirrel, and some mice as pets. Since she often helped her father with some of his easier duties, she knew how miserable Toad was.

One day, she said to her father, "I can't bear to see that poor beast so unhappy and getting so thin. Let me try to take care of him. I'm so used to animals that I probably can get him to eat."

The old jailer agreed, since he was annoyed with Toad's sulking and fancy airs.

That very day, the girl knocked at the door to Toad's cell and went in. "Cheer up and be sensible, Toad," she said. "You must eat, and I've brought you some of my own dinner. It's beef and cabbage, fresh from the oven."

Even though Toad refused to touch a bite and remained stretched out on the dungeon floor, wailing and kicking his legs until after the girl had gone, the wonderful smell of the freshly cooked food stayed in his nostrils and soon reached his brain. And his brain began to work, thinking new thoughts of his old life, his old friends, and his own great cleverness.

He suddenly came alive! "Why, I can do anything if I set my mind to it, even escape from

The Smell Soon Reached His Brain.

here! Yes, I must plan for that."

Hours later, the girl returned, this time with a tray of steaming tea and hot buttered toast. This food reminded Toad of the wonderful meals he had been served at Toad Hall, and this time he sat up, munching the toast, sipping the tea, and talking about his house, his friends, and, of course, his own importance.

The girl saw that Toad's spirits were lifted when he talked about himself, and she encouraged him to go on. And he did, giving her details about Toad Hall and descriptions of all his animal friends. By the time she left the cell that evening, Toad had returned to his former self, even singing a song before he curled up on his straw and fell into a dreamy sleep.

In the days that followed, the girl and Toad had many interesting talks. The girl grew very sorry for Toad, for he was a poor little animal who had been locked up in prison for a very minor offense.

Then one morning, the girl came in with an

Many Interesting Talks

announcement. "Toad, I have an aunt who is a washerwoman."

"That's nothing you have to be ashamed of," answered Toad. "*I* have several aunts who *should be* washerwomen."

"Do be quiet, Toad. You talk too much. Just listen to me for a minute. This aunt does washing for all the prisoners in this jail. She takes it out Monday morning and brings it back Friday evening. It occurred to me that since you're very rich and she's very poor, you could help each other, *if* she were approached in the right way."

Toad didn't understand what the girl was getting at, but he urged, "Go on, my dear."

"My plan is for you to arrange to have her dress and bonnet, and you could escape from the jail in them. You two have figures that are very much alike."

"I beg your pardon," said Toad in a huff. "I happen to have a very elegant figure, for a Toad, that is."

"I Have an Aunt Who Is a Washerwoman."

"So has my aunt. But have it your way, you horrible, proud, ungrateful animal! I'm just sorry I even tried to help you!"

"Thank you very much anyway," said Toad. "But really, you can't expect Mr. Toad of Toad Hall to go about the countryside disguised as a washerwoman."

"Then you can rot here dressed as a Toad!" shouted the girl. "You can hardly ride out of here in a coach with four horses!"

On some occasions, Toad had been known to admit that he was wrong, and this was one of them. "You're a kind, clever girl, and I'm a proud, stupid Toad," he confessed. "Please, introduce me to your deserving aunt. I'm certain we can come to a satisfactory agreement for both of us."

The next evening, which was Friday, the girl brought her aunt into Toad's cell. The woman knew what was about to happen, and the sight of Toad's gold coins on the table left very little for them to talk about. In return for his money,

Toad's Gold Coins

Toad got a cotton print dress, an apron, a shawl, and a faded black bonnet.

The woman asked only one favor. "Please tie me up and gag me and leave me in a corner of the cell. This way, I can claim that you attacked me and I won't lose my job or get in trouble."

Toad was delighted. "I'd be happy to do that for you, good woman." Then to himself, he added, "I'm also doing myself a favor by upholding my reputation as a desperate and dangerous fellow! How marvelous!"

Once the washerwoman was tied up in a corner, the girl helped Toad out of his vest and jacket and into the dress and apron and shawl and bonnet. "You're the very picture of my aunt!" giggled the girl.

Toad frowned. He felt insulted, but was wise enough not to say a word.

The girl hugged him and gently pushed him towards the cell door. "Good-bye, Toad, and good luck. You'll be passing the guards on the

"The Very Picture of My Aunt!"

way out, and they'll probably tease you. They always tease my aunt since she's a widow woman. But just tease them back and you'll have no trouble getting through."

Toad's heart was beating rapidly as he set out on what he considered a hare-brained adventure, but he soon found that the girl's advice worked perfectly. The little washerwoman in the print dress found every door open for her as she left the prison. Toad even managed to avoid the arms of one guard who wanted a kiss from the widowed washerwoman!

Minutes later, he found himself breathing in the fresh air of the outside world. He was free!

Dizzy with the success of his daring escape, Toad walked quickly towards the lights of the town. "I can't stay there too long," he told himself, "for people in town surely know the real washerwoman."

Some red and green lights off to the side of town caught his attention. "Aha! What luck! There's a railroad station—the very thing I

He Was Free!

need at this moment."

Once he reached the station, Toad checked the schedule posted on the wall. A train was due in half an hour and would be heading in the direction of Toad Hall. "More luck!" he cried happily.

He went up to the ticket window and told the clerk where he wanted to go. Then, as was his habit, he put his fingers to where his vest pocket would have been, to reach for his money. But all his fingers touched were a cotton dress and apron. There were no pockets and no money.

"Good heavens!" he thought. "I left my money and keys and watch, everything that's usually in my pocket, back at the jail when I changed clothes." But even in this situation, and with other travelers getting impatient in the line behind him, Toad tried to use his old airs of importance to persuade the clerk to give him a ticket.

"Look here, old chap, it seems I've left my

No Pockets and No Money

purse behind. Just give me the ticket and I'll send the money on tomorrow. I'm quite well known in these parts."

The ticket clerk stared at him and at the faded bonnet. then laughed. "Your game won't work on me. madam. There's no free rides given here. Now move aside. You're holding up the other passengers in the line."

Baffled and full of despair. Toad wandered down the platform alongside the train. Tears ran down his cheeks as he moaned. "How awful to be so close to safety, so close to home and to be stopped because I don't have a few shillings to pay my fare! My escape will be discovered soon, and then the police will be after me again. What am I to do?"

As he came alongside the engine, he saw a big, burly man in uniform oiling the train. The man turned to the weeping woman in the print dress and faded bonnet and asked, "What's the trouble, little mother?"

"Oh, sir! I'm a poor washerwoman who's lost

Tears Ran Down His Cheeks.

her money. I *must* get home tonight to my children and I don't know how I can."

"Well, I tell you what I'll do," said the kindly engineer. "You're a washerwoman and I'm an engine driver who dirties lots of shirts. If you'll wash some for me when you get home and send them along to the station, I'll give you a ride on my engine. It's against company rules, but there's no one checking way out here in these parts."

Toad's misery quickly turned to joy and he climbed up into the cab of the engine. He promised himself that once he was back home, he'd send the engineer enough money to pay any washerwoman to do his shirts.

Soon, the train was moving out of the station. Toad was so overjoyed at the thought of speeding closer to Toad Hall, to his friends, to his money, to his soft bed, and to the praise he'd receive for his clever escape, that he began to sing and dance all around the cab.

The engineer looked on in amazement. "I've

He Climbed Up Into the Cab.

seen some strange washerwomen before," he mumbled, "but never one like this!"

Several miles later, the engineer climbed onto the coals and looked back behind the train. "We're the last train running tonight," he told Toad, "but I could swear I heard another train following us. . . . Yes, I see it now. . . . It's speeding along. Seems to be chasing us!"

Toad had stopped his dancing and was now crouching in the coals, desperate to do something, but not knowing what.

"They're gaining on us fast!" called the engineer. "And the engine is filled with policemen waving sticks and swords and revolvers, and shouting 'Stop! Stop!'"

Toad fell to his knees and pleaded, "Save me, dear, kind Mr. Engineer, and I'll confess to everything. I'm not a washerwoman. I am a toad, the well-known Mr. Toad of Toad Hall. I've just escaped—through my own cleverness, of course—from a horrible dungeon where I

"They're Gaining on Us Fast!"

was unjustly imprisoned. If those fellows on that engine capture me again, it will mean the end for me."

"What were you imprisoned for?"

"Nothing really much. I borrowed a motor-car. I didn't mean to steal it, but judges don't understand that."

"You've been a naughty toad, and I really ought to let the police have you. But you seem to be so distressed, and I'm so soft-hearted when I see an animal in tears that I *will* help you. Now, cheer up and we'll beat them yet!"

The two piled more coals into the furnace and the engine leaped forward. Still, the police were gaining on them.

"They have a better engine that can catch us," said the engineer. "There's only one thing left to try. It's your only chance, so listen carefully. Up ahead is a long tunnel. On the other side of the tunnel, thick woods line both sides of the tracks. I'll put on all the speed I can while we go through the tunnel. They'll prob-

More Coals Into the Furnace

ably slow down, since they're not familiar with it. When we're out on the other side of the tunnel, I'll put on the brakes real fast. The moment we stop, jump out and hide in the woods before they come through the tunnel and see you. Then I'll go full-speed again and let them chase me as long as they like and as far as they like."

Toad nodded eagerly and followed the engineer's orders. When he heard the call, "Now, jump!" Toad did. He rolled down a short embankment, picked himself up, unhurt, and scrambled into the woods to hide.

From behind a tree, he saw his train pick up speed and the other engine come roaring out of the tunnel. When both had passed, Toad began to laugh and laugh hard—the first time he had done so since he had been thrown into prison.

But his laughter didn't last long when he realized that it was quite dark and quite cold. He had no money, nothing to eat, and no place

"Now, Jump!"

to spend the night. Even the woods seemed un-
friendly, with owls laughing at him and foxes
passing him with sarcastic remarks about his
washerwoman clothes.

Finally, after hours of wandering, the cold,
hungry, tired Toad found a hollow tree. He
made himself a bed with leaves and branches,
and soon fell soundly asleep till the next morning.

Toad Made Himself a Bed.

Confident, Though a Little Hungry

CHAPTER 8

Toad's Adventures

The sun streaming into the hollow on that early summer morning woke Toad. At first, he looked around for the stone walls and little barred window of his cell. Then he remembered where he was and how he got there.

Shaking the dry leaves out of his hair, he crept out of the hollow and marched off, confident and hopeful, though a little hungry. He crossed several fields until he came to a road. Perhaps he'd meet someone who could tell him which way to go.

Soon, the road began to run alongside a

canal. At a bend, Toad came upon a horse plodding along. A rope was attached to his collar and its other end was attached to a barge slowly making its way down the middle of the canal. Steering the barge at the tiller was a big fat woman wearing a linen sun-bonnet.

"A nice morning, ma'am!" called the woman as she spotted Toad on the shore.

"I'm in luck!" thought Toad. Then he twisted his face into a sad, gloomy expression as he called back, "It probably *is* a nice morning, ma'am, but not for a washer-woman who's in trouble like I am. My married daughter sent for me. An emergency, the message said. Well, if you're a mother too, you can understand that I had to go at once, even though it meant leaving my other young children home alone. As if that wasn't bad enough, I've lost my money and my way too."

"Where does your married daughter live?"

"Near River Bank, close to a fine house they call Toad Hall. Do you know it?"

Steering the Barge

"Know it? Why, it's only a few miles ahead. I'm going that way myself and I'd be glad to give you a lift in my barge."

Toad was overjoyed! "I always come out on top!" he thought as the woman steered the barge to shore and he hopped on board.

"So you're a washerwoman," said the barge-woman politely. "I hear it's a very good business."

"Finest business in the country!" boasted Toad. "I have only wealthy customers who appreciate my washing and ironing talents."

"You sound *very* fond of washing."

"Oh, I love it! I'm at my happiest when both my arms are deep in soapy water!"

"Then it's lucky for both of us that we met," said the woman, rubbing her chin thoughtfully.

Toad suddenly became nervous. "What do you mean?" he asked.

"Well, *I* like washing too, but I've got this barge to run since my husband's too lazy to do

158

Toad Hopped On Board.

it. I simply can't think of anything but the wash that's piling up in the cabin. . . . Say, since you say you're happiest when your arms are in soapy water, you can help me out and be happy at the same time. It'll be more fun for you than just sitting here looking at the shore."

Toad was now thoroughly frightened. "Let *me* steer!" he said. "Then you can do your own washing. I wouldn't want to spoil your things by not doing them the way you like."

"Let *you* steer? It takes practice to steer a barge properly. Besides, it's dull work, and I want you to be happy after all your family troubles."

Toad was cornered. He thought of jumping off the barge, but he was too far from the bank. "I guess if I'm desperate enough, I *can* wash. Probably any fool can do it."

So he went into the cabin for the tub and soap, and began to wash, or what he thought washing was. After a long half-hour, he was

What He Thought Washing Was

getting angrier and angrier. Nothing he did could get the clothes clean, not rubbing, not slapping, not punching. Nothing!

By now, his back was aching from bending over the tub, and his paws were getting all crinkly and shriveled up from being in the water all that time. As he lost the soap for the fiftieth time, he began muttering under his breath words that neither a washerwoman nor a Toad should ever mutter!

A burst of laughter from the barge-woman made him straighten up. "I've been watching you all this time," she cackled, "and it's just as I thought—you're a fake! You've never washed a thing in your entire life!"

Toad's anger finally boiled over and he shrieked, "How dare you talk to your superiors like that! I'll have you know I'm the highly respected, distinguished Mr. Toad, and I will *not* be laughed at by a common barge-woman like you!"

"Well, no horrid, crawly Toad is going to stay

"You're A Fake!"

on my nice clean barge!" she cried as she let go of the tiller and grabbed Toad by one front leg and one hind leg.

The next moment, Toad found himself flying through the air. He landed in the water with a loud splash, then rose to the surface choking for air. He looked back and saw the woman laughing. "I'll get even with you!" he vowed. "I don't know how, but I will!"

His long dress slowed the swim to shore, and he had to rest before climbing up the steep bank with the wet skirt over his arms. Once on the path, he started to run after the barge, wild with desire for revenge!

The barge-woman was still laughing and shouting out taunts, but Toad didn't waste his time or words. He wanted *real* revenge, and he saw his chance for it just up ahead—it was the horse!

He quickly overtook the slow, plodding horse and untied the tow-rope that attached it to the barge. Then he jumped on the animal's back,

Flying Through The Air

gave it a vigorous kick in the sides, and gal-loped off.

He left the path and headed for open coun-try, looking back only once. The barge had run aground on the other side of the canal, and the woman was waving her arms and shouting wildly for him to stop. But Toad only laughed as he urged the horse on to greater speed.

After traveling several miles, Toad reached an open field with a few scattered trees. Under one tree stood an shabby gypsy wagon. Beside it sat a man smoking a pipe and stirring an iron pot hung over a fire.

Gurgling sounds from the pot traveled to Toad's ears, and warm, rich smells flew into his nostrils, reminding him how hungry he was.

The man lifted his eyes from the pot and stared at the woman on horseback. "Care to sell that horse of yours?" he asked.

For the moment, Toad was stunned. Then he realized that the horse could bring him two

He Urged The Horse On.

things he wanted and needed desperately—
money and food. But he'd have to be shrewd!

"What!" he cried, pretending to be shocked
and insulted. "Me sell this beautiful young
horse of mine? No, it's out of the question. I
need him to carry my washing to my customers, and besides, I'm too fond of him. . . . All
the same, how much would you offer if I *were*
interested in selling him?"

"Four shillings."

"I'm afraid not, my man. Four shillings is an
insult for this beautiful young horse."

"Well, I can make it five, but that's all the
animal's worth. Five's my last offer."

Toad thought long and hard. He was hungry
and penniless, and still far from home. Even
now, the police might be searching for him. He
reasoned to himself, "While five shillings isn't
very much for a horse, it didn't cost me anything to get him, so whatever I make is clear
profit!" Then he spoke firmly to the gypsy. "I
tell you what I'll do, and this is *my* last word.

"How Much Would You Offer?"

You give me six shillings and as much food as I can possibly eat at one meal from that iron pot of yours. If that's not agreeable, I'll be on my way." The gypsy grumbled, but finally pulled a dirty cloth bag from his pocket and counted out six shillings into Toad's paw. Then he climbed into his wagon and came back out with a large plate and a fork and spoon.

Tilting the iron pot, he dished out the most beautiful stew Toad had even seen or smelled or tasted. Toad actually cried with joy as he ate, emptying his plate four times and asking for more each time.

When his stomach could hold no more food, Toad said good-bye to the gypsy and to the horse. After the gypsy gave him directions to River Bank, he set off. "How clever I've been to fool everyone! Nothing can go wrong now!" he told himself. "The sun is shining, my wet clothes are dry, I have money in my pocket, I'm near my home and my friends and safety, and best of all, my stomach is nice and stuffed with

When His Stomach Could Hold No More

a hot, nourishing meal!"

Yes, Toad felt big and strong and self-confident, and he made up a song that he sang at the top of his voice as he tramped along:

"The world has held great heroes,
As history books have showed;
But never a name will have the fame
Of the clever Mr. Toad!"

On and on he went, making up new verses, all boasting about himself, all adding to his conceit and pride.

After many miles on country lanes, Toad reached a main road. A cloud of dust in the distance was coming towards him, and with the dust came a familiar pop-pop that filled Toad with joy.

"A motorcar! How wonderful!" thought Toad. "I'll have to make up a story that will convince them to give me a lift, and who knows? Maybe I'll even *drive* up to Toad Hall! That would make Badger sit up and take notice!"

So Toad stepped out into the middle of the

He Made Up A Song.

road and waved at the approaching car. When it was close enough for him to see it clearly, he began to shake violently. Then he doubled up and collapsed right where he was standing. For he recognized the car as the very same one he had stolen from the inn!

"It's all over!" Toad cried miserably. "Prison again! Chains again! What a fool I've been! Why did I ever strut across the countryside during the day, singing such conceited songs! I should have hidden in the woods and traveled only at night!"

The motorcar drew closer, then stopped. Two gentlemen got out and walked towards the crumbled, miserable creature lying in the road.

"Oh, dear! How sad!" said one of the men. "It looks like a washerwoman has fainted!"

"Let's lift her into the car and take her to the nearest village," said the other.

So they gently placed Toad in the back seat and propped him up with cushions.

The Very Same One He Had Stolen!

"They didn't recognize me!" thought Toad gleefully as they started up again. And he opened one eye, then the other.

"Look!" said one man. "She looks better already. Must be the fresh air."

"Yes, I am a bit better," said Toad weakly. "But I was thinking that perhaps if I sat in the front seat, beside the driver, I could get more air in my face. Then I'm sure I'd be perfectly fine again."

"That's a sensible idea," said one man. And they helped Toad into the front seat, while the passenger went into the back.

Toad was now full of confidence again, and the old yearning to be behind the wheel overpowered him once more. "Please, sir," he said to the driver beside him, "I'd like to drive the car for a little while. I've been watching you, and it looks so easy. And I'd be able to tell my friends that once I drove a motorcar!"

The driver hesitated, but his friend exclaimed, "I like her spirit! Let her have a try.

He Opened One Eye, Then The Other.

She can't do any harm, and you'll be beside her to look after her."

So the driver got out and came around to the passenger seat while Toad slid over and eagerly grabbed the steering wheel. He pretended to listen respectfully to the instructions the man was giving him, then he slowly and carefully started to drive.

At first, the men clapped their hands at the little washerwoman's skill. Then Toad began to speed up. Faster and faster and faster, he went, ignoring the men's warning shouts.

The driver tried to lean over to grab the wheel. "Stop, washerwoman!" he cried.

But Toad elbowed him out of the way and speeded up even more. "Washerwoman, indeed!" shouted Toad. "Why, I am Toad, the motorcar thief, the escaped prisoner! Sit back and learn what driving really is, in the hands of the famous, skillful, fearless Toad!"

With a cry of horror, the enraged men jumped up and flung themselves on Toad,

Toad Grabbed the Steering Wheel.

forgetting for the moment that they were in a speeding car. Toad turned to avoid them and sent the car crashing off the road and into the thick mud of a pond.

Toad found himself flying through the air, feeling for a moment like a graceful bird, until he landed on some soft grass in a meadow. He picked himself up and began running away. He glanced back quickly and saw the car sinking. The two men were floundering in the water with their long coats pulling them down.

Toad continued to run as hard as he could, through hedges, over ditches, across fields, until he was sure he was out of sight and not being followed. Then he sat down to rest and catch his breath.

As his confidence returned, he began to giggle. "Ha! Ha! As usual, Toad has come out on top! I got them to give me a ride, to put me in the front seat, and to let me drive! And *I* was the one who escaped from the pond unhurt, while those foolish men got stuck in the mud!

He Saw the Car Sinking.

What a clever Toad I am! What a great, great Toad—"

Just then, a slight noise in the distance behind him made him turn his head. "Oh, no! Oh, misery! Oh, horror!" he cried. "The police are coming after me!"

Toad sprang to his feet and began to run. "Oh, my!" he panted. "What an *idiot* I am! What a conceited, mindless idiot!"

The men were gaining on him. In his panic, Toad began running blindly and wildly. When he turned to look back, his feet suddenly left the ground and he found himself in the air for a brief second. Then splash! He was dropping into deep rushing water, into a river that was carrying him along in its swiftly flowing current.

Toad tried to grab onto the reeds that grew along the bank, but the river kept pulling him away. "Oh, my!" he gasped. "If I ever steal—" But the river pulled him under before he could make another empty promise.

The River Kept Pulling Him Away.

He popped up to the surface, breathless and weak. The current was now pushing him towards a big dark hole just above the water level in the bank. He reached up with a gasp and grabbed on to the edge, then slowly and painfully pulled himself up until his elbows were resting there. He dropped his head into his hands and held on, puffing and panting until his breath returned.

Suddenly, from inside that dark hole came two shiny circles. As they came closer, a face appeared around them: A small brown face with whiskers and neat ears and silky hair. It was a familiar face. It was Rat!

It Was a Familiar Face.

Up Out of the Water

CHAPTER 9

No Home To Come Home To

Rat's little brown paw grabbed Toad by the back of his neck and hauled him up out of the water and over the edge of the hole into his front hall.

Mud, weeds, and water dripped off Toad as he cried, "Oh, Ratty! I've been through such suffering, such escapes, such disguises. But I bore all these trials so nobly! I proved to everyone just how smart a Toad I really am! Just wait till I tell you of my thrilling adventures and just how clever I—"

Rat didn't let him continue. "Toad," he said

firmly, "go upstairs at once and take off that rag that makes you look like a washerwoman. Then clean yourself thoroughly and put on some of my clothes. You may come back down when you look like a gentleman, if that's possible."

Toad didn't like being ordered around, and he was about to argue back, but he saw himself in the mirror and changed his mind.

By the time he came back down, cleaned and dressed properly, his pride and conceit had returned. He told Rat all that had happened to him, boasting of his cleverness and cunning rather than admitting his foolishness and guilt. He even made it sound like an exciting adventure!

When Toad was finally talked out, Rat sighed and said, "Now, Toady, I know you've been through a lot of pain already, but don't you see what a fool you've been making of yourself? Handcuffed! Imprisoned! Chased! Starved! Terrified! Insulted! Jeered at! And

His Pride and Conceit Returned.

even flung into the water by a woman! That's *not* an adventure! And it's all because you stole a motorcar, which you can easily afford to buy yourself!"

"You're right, Ratty. I've been conceited and foolish, but from now on I'm going to be a good Toad and not bring any more shame on my friends or myself. I'll go down to Toad Hall now, get into my own clothes, and pick up my life again. I think I've had enough adventures to last me the rest of my life!"

"Go down to Toad Hall?" cried Rat. "You mean you haven't heard?"

"Heard what?" gasped Toad, turning pale.

"The stoats and weasels and ferrets from the Wild Wood have captured Toad Hall!"

Tears filled Toad's eyes and splashed onto the table. "Go on, Ratty, tell me all about it," he sobbed. "I can bear it."

"Well, when you got into all that trouble and were thrown in jail, Mole and Badger and I stuck up for you. We believed you had been

Wild Wood Animals Captured Toad Hall.

unfairly treated and would somehow come back to us. But all the animals in the Wild Wood said you deserved everything you got and you'd never, never come back again!"

"Those beasts!" cried Toad.

"Anyhow, Mole and Badger decided to move into Toad Hall to guard it and keep it clean and ready for you when you returned. Now, here's the painful and tragic part of my story. One dark, stormy night, a gang of bloodthirsty weasels, ferrets, and stoats broke down the doors and rushed at Mole and Badger from all sides. Our faithful friends tried to put up a fight, but they were only two against hundreds. They were badly beaten with sticks and thrown out into the storm."

"Oh, my poor friends!" sobbed Toad.

"Then those Wild Wooders took over Toad Hall and have been living there ever since, sleeping away half the day, eating your food, drinking your fine wines, making a terrible mess, and boasting to everyone, 'We're here

"Those Wild Wooders Took Over."

for good!' "

"Well, we'll see about that!" exclaimed Toad, getting up and reaching for a stick.

"That won't do any good, Toady. You'll only get into more trouble," warned Rat.

But Toad was off, marching quickly down the road, fuming and muttering in anger. No sooner was he at the front gate of Toad Hall than a long, yellow ferret popped out from behind a post and pointed a gun at him.

"Who comes here?" demanded the ferret. "How dare you talk to me like that! Come out at once or I'll—"

The ferret raised his gun to his shoulder and sent a bullet whistling over Toad's head. Then he burst out laughing as Toad scampered off down the road as fast as his legs could carry him.

"I warned you!" said Rat when Toad had returned. "They've got armed guards posted everywhere. You simply must wait!"

But Toad wasn't much good at waiting, and

"Who Comes Here?"

that afternoon, he took out Rat's boat and set off up the river towards Toad Hall. Just as he was passing under the bridge at the entrance to the creek . . . Crash!

A huge rock dropped from above and smashed through the bottom of the boat. The little boat quickly filled with water and sank.

"It'll be your head next time, Toady!" called two stoats, who were leaning over the bridge and laughing as Toad struggled to shore and headed back to Rat's home.

"I told you not to go!" said Rat angrily. "And this time you've lost my boat and ruined my nice suit. Really, Toad, this is hardly the way to keep friends!"

"You're absolutely right, Ratty. And I'm truly sorry. I've been headstrong and willful. From now on, I won't do anything without your advice and approval. I promise."

"I hope you mean that. But we can't do anything until we see Mole and Badger."

"Yes, of course! What's become of them?"

A Huge Rock Dropped From Above.

"Those two devoted friends have been camping out in all kinds of weather, watching over your house and planning how to get it back for you. You don't deserve such true and loyal friends!"

"I'm an ungrateful beast, I know," sobbed Toad. "Let me go out and find them and share their hard life...after dinner, of course."

Rat couldn't refuse to serve Toad a good dinner, since his friend had been living on prison food for such a long time.

Just as they were finishing their meal, Badger and Mole came in. Both looked shabby and unwashed, covered with mud and hay.

Badger came up to Toad and they shook hands. "Welcome home, Toad. Sorry this has to be such a sad homecoming." Then he sat down at the table and served himself some food.

Toad was upset that Badger could think of food at a time like this, but Mole's greeting lifted his spirits.

"How wonderful to have you back again!"

"And Share Their Hard Life . . . After Dinner."

cried Mole, dancing around him. "How ever did you manage to escape, you clever Toad?"

"I'm not really clever. I just broke out of the strongest prison in all England, captured a railway train and escaped on it, disguised myself and traveled across the country, fooling everybody I could. That's all there was to it."

"That sounds exciting! Suppose you tell me everything while I eat," said Mole.

"I think it's more important for us to learn what's happening at Toad Hall," interrupted Rat. "Toad's stories can wait."

"Everything's as bad as ever," said Mole glumly. "Guards are still posted everywhere, guns are continuously poked at us, stones are thrown at us, and the animals are always laughing at us."

"Well, I think Toad ought to—" Rat began.

"No, he oughtn't!" snapped Mole.

"Well, I won't do it, whatever it is!" yelled Toad.

By now, Toad, Mole, and Rat were shouting

"What's Happening at Toad Hall?"

together and the noise was deafening.

Suddenly, a soft, firm voice spoke. "Be quiet, all of you!"

Badger had finished his meal and was looking at them sternly. All three quieted down. He got up from his chair and stood before the fireplace. Pointing his finger at Toad, he said, "You are a troublesome little animal and you should be ashamed of yourself! What do you think your father, who was my old friend, would have said if he had known what you've done?"

Toad threw himself down on the sofa, rolled his legs over his face, and began to sob.

"Stop crying," said Badger gently. "We're going to forget the past and make a new beginning. Now, what Mole says is true. The stoats guarding Toad Hall are the best sentinels in the world. We could never attack the place. But there are ways of getting it back besides taking it by storm. And I'm going to share that secret with you."

"Be Quiet, All of You!"

Toad sat up and dried his eyes. Secrets were exciting things for him because he could never keep one and because he got a special thrill out of telling a secret he had promised not to tell.

Badger continued. "There's an underground passage that leads from the river bank right near here and comes up in the middle of Toad Hall."

"That's nonsense!" snapped Toad. "I know every inch of the place and there's nothing of the sort underground. Take my word!"

"My young friend," insisted Badger, "your father was a fine man who told me many more things than he would ever dream of telling you. This passage had been made hundreds of years before he ever came to live at Toad Hall. When he discovered it, he cleaned it out and repaired it just in case danger forced him or his family to use it. And he told me specifically, 'Don't let my son know about it. He's a good boy, but he loves to talk. If he's ever in trouble and needs to use it, you can tell him about it.

"There's an Underground Passage."

But not before!' "

Toad frowned at first, then, like the good fellow he really was at heart, he quickly brightened. "Perhaps my father was right. I *am* a bit of a talker, especially when my friends are gathered around me. But do go on, Badger. How will this passage help us?"

"I found out that there's going to be a big party tomorrow night at Toad Hall to celebrate the Chief Weasel's birthday. Everyone will be in the banquet hall eating and drinking. They won't suspect anything, so they won't be armed. Besides, they trust their guards to protect them."

"But how will we get past the guards?" asked Rat.

"That's where the passage comes in. It comes up right under the butler's pantry, next to the banquet hall," explained Badger.

"We'll creep quietly into the pantry and rush them!" cried Mole. "What a surprise!"

"And whack 'em and whack 'em!" shouted

"I Am a Bit of a talker."

Toad, running and jumping around the room.

"Our plan is settled then," said Badger. "Now you must all go to bed. We'll make the final arrangements in the morning."

Toad obeyed, though he thought he was much too excited to sleep. Still, once his head hit the pillow, his dreams carried him into secret passages and to a triumphant return to Toad Hall.

It was late when Toad awoke the next morning. The other animals had already finished their breakfast. Badger was sitting in an armchair reading the paper, and Rat was preparing piles of weapons for that evening's attack.

Just then, Mole came tumbling into the room, proudly announcing, "I just returned from having fun teasing those stoats guarding Toad Hall. I put on that old washerwoman dress Toad came home in yesterday—it had been washed, of course—along with the apron and bonnet and shawl, and off I went.

"'Good morning' says I to the guards, bold

His Dreams Carried Him to Secret Passages.

as could be, but very respectful. 'Want any washing done today?'

" 'Go away, washerwoman!' they called back. 'We don't wash, not ever! Now run away!'

"Well, says I to them, 'Run away, you say? It won't be me that'll be running away very soon!' "

Badger put down his paper to listen to Mole's story.

"Well, the sergeant tells 'em, 'Never mind *her*! She doesn't know what she's saying!'

" 'Oh, don't I?' says I. 'Well, let me tell you this. My daughter washes for Mr. Badger, and she told me that over *one hundred* bloodthirsty badgers, armed with rifles, are going to attack Toad Hall tonight through the stables. And six boat-loads of rats, with pistols and cutlasses, will come up the river and land in the garden. Then a select body of toads, who call them-selves Death-or-Glory Toads, will storm the french doors screaming for vengeance. I don't suppose there'll be much left of you to wash by

Badger Put Down His Paper.

the time they're done with you!'

"Then I ran away. But I hid behind a hedge to see what would happen. Those stoats were as nervous as could be, running all around, falling over each other, and giving orders that no one paid attention to. Then I heard the sergeant say, 'That's just like the weasels! They're going to be enjoying their party, while we have to stand guard and be cut to pieces by bloodthirsty badgers!' "

"Oh, Mole, you imbecile!" cried Toad. "You warned them! Now you've spoiled everything!"

"Mole," said Badger quietly, "you have more sense in your little finger than some animals have in the whole of their fat little bodies!" And he turned to give Toad a nasty look. Then he continued. "Mole, you have been quite clever. I'm proud of you."

Toad was wild with jealousy, especially because he couldn't figure out what Mole had done that was so clever. But before he could show a temper or protest, Rat announced

"But I Hid Behind a Hedge."

lunch. And Toad would never miss a meal!

Once they were finished, Badger took a nap to rest up for the attack that evening and Rat continued adding to his piles of weapons. Mole led Toad out into the garden and made him recount all his adventures, which Toad was only too eager to do, especially since Mole was a wonderful listener and no one would be around to check the truthfulness of his stories or criticize them.

His Pile of Weapons

Dressed for Battle

CHAPTER 10

A Changed Toad

That evening, Rat brought Badger, Mole, and Toad into the parlor and dressed them for battle. He buckled a belt around each animal and stuck into it a sword, a cutlass, a pair of pistols, a club, several sets of handcuffs, some bandages, a canteen with water, and some sandwiches.

Badger laughed good-naturedly at these preparations and held up his own big, thick stick. "I know you mean well, Ratty, but all I need is this stick to do what I have to."

"*Please*, Badger! I don't want to be blamed

for forgetting *anything*! Now, let's go!"

Badger picked up a lantern, raised his stick above his head, and called, "Follow me! Mole first, 'cause I'm pleased with him, Rat next, and Toad last. And, Toady, you'd better not make a sound!"

Toad sulked as he got at the end of the line. "What's so special about Moley!" he muttered. "I'm much cleverer than he!"

The animals set off, with Badger leading them along the river. Then he suddenly swung over the edge of the bank and dropped into a hole. Mole and Rat followed quickly, but sulking, clumsy Toad managed to slip and fall into the water. His loud splash and cry of fear stopped the others, and they turned back to pull him out.

"If there's any more of your foolishness, Toad, I'll leave you behind!" Badger warned. Then he signaled for them to continue on as the hole led into a dark, narrow tunnel.

As they made their way along the tunnel,

"Follow Me!"

Toad began to shiver, partly from fear and partly from being soaked to his skin. When he began lagging behind, Rat called out, "Come on, Toad! Come on!"

Frightened at being left behind and alone, Toad "came on" so quickly that he ran into Rat, who ran into Mole, who ran into Badger. There was such confusion, with everyone thinking they were being attacked, that Toad barely escaped being hit by a bullet from Badger's pistol.

By now, Badger was ready to leave Toad behind, but Rat and Mole promised to watch him and keep him between them. They groped along until they heard sounds overhead.

"We're under the banquet hall now," said Badger. "You can hear the weasels and ferrets shouting and stomping their feet and pounding their fists on the table. With all that noise, they'll never hear us. Come on!"

Moments later, Badger stopped and pointed up. "Here's the trap door to the butler's pantry.

"There Was Such Confusion."

Let's put our shoulders to it and push it back."

Soon, the door was opened and the four friends climbed up into the pantry. Only a door separated them from the banquet hall, and the noise coming from it was deafening.

When the shouting and cheering quieted down a little, a voice the animals recognized as the Chief Weasel's began to speak. "Thank you, friends." - (cheers) - "I'd like to say a kind word . . ." - (applause) - " . . . about our good host, Mr. Toad!" - (great laughter) - "*Good* Toad! *Modest* Toad! *Honest* Toad!" - (shrieks of merriment).

"Let me at him!" muttered Toad, gritting his teeth.

"Just wait!" said Badger, holding him back. "You'll get to him soon enough. Now, get ready, everyone!" Then taking a firm grip on his big stick, Badger cried out, "The hour has come! Follow me!"

He flung the door open, and the attackers raced into the banquet hall, the mighty Bad-

The Chief Weasel Began to Speak.

ger with his great stick swinging above his head, the grim Mole thrusting his sword in front of him, the determined Rat with a pistol in each hand, and the frenzied Toad leaping in the air and shrieking horrifying Toad-whoops.

Oh, the squealing and squeaking and screeching that followed! The terrified weasels dove under the tables and sprang toward the windows. The frantic ferrets rushed wildly for the fireplace and jammed themselves into the chimney. Tables and chairs overturned! Glass and china crashed to the floor! Food splattered on walls and floors!

The battle was over in minutes. The four heroes strode up and down the hall, whacking at any head that still moved. The room was cleared, with the exception of a few weasels stretched out on the floor. These prisoners were being handcuffed by Mole.

Badger leaned on his stick and called to Mole, "You were simply great, my friend. Now,

Into the Banquet Hall!

I think you ought to run along outside and see what those guards are doing. Between hearing your washerwoman's warning today and seeing the animals fleeing the hall tonight, they probably won't be giving us any more trouble."

While Badger, Rat, and Toad began cleaning up the room and preparing some dinner for themselves, Mole hurried out. He wasn't gone more than a few minutes when he returned with an armful of rifles, which he dumped on the floor.

"It's all over," he reported with a broad smile. "From what I can make out, some of the stoats were already nervous and jumpy when the attack began. They dropped their rifles and fled when they heard the shrieks and yells from inside the hall. The other stoats stayed at their posts for a while, but when the weasels and ferrets came running out, the stoats feared they were being attacked. So they all began wrestling and punching and rolling over each other until they all rolled into the river.

"It's All Over."

Every one of them! But these are their rifles."

"Excellent! You're a fine animal!" said Badger. "Now, let's all sit down to our victory dinner!"

Being a gentleman, Toad put aside his conceit and jealousy, and added, "Thank you kindly, dear Mole, for all your efforts tonight and especially for your cleverness this morning."

"That's my brave Toad!" beamed Badger. "You know, Toad, you really should host a banquet for all of River Bank to celebrate this victory. And it should be as early as tomorrow night. We'll take care of all the arrangements in the morning, but you'll need to write the invitations."

Toad didn't like being told what to do. "I don't want to spend my first morning back at Toad Hall writing some silly invitations. It was your idea, Badger, so *you* make all the arrange—"

Then suddenly, a twinkle appeared in Toad's eyes. "No, I'll do it, of course. It's all in the

"Our Victory Dinner"

name of friendship."

Badger looked at Toad suspiciously. "He's up to something," he thought. "I'd better keep an eye on him."

That night, they all slept at Toad Hall, in the fine, clean beds that their prisoners had been forced to prepare for them.

After breakfast the following morning, Toad hurried to his desk and began writing out his invitations.

"How clever I am!" he thought gleefully. "I can use the invitations to tell everyone how bravely I fought to recapture my home, how I personally drove the Chief Weasel out, and I can mention my triumphs while I was gone. Oh, what a wonderful opportunity this is! And I'll even prepare a program for the evening, with a welcoming speech by Toad, with songs by Toad, and with a closing speech by Toad."

When the invitations were finished, Toad called in one of the weasel prisoners Mole had released. Beaming with pride at having out-

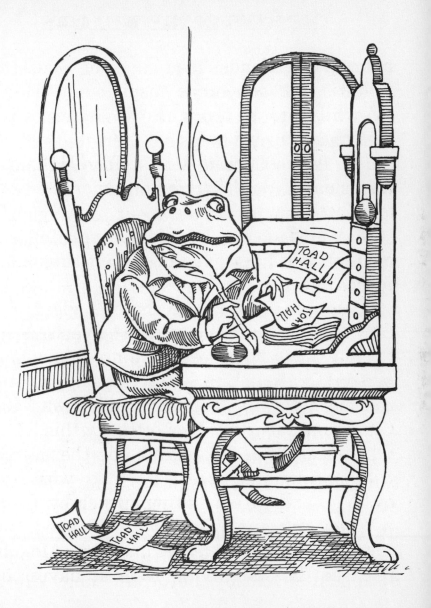

Toad Began Writing His Invitations.

smarted his friends, Toad gave the weasel his invitations to deliver.

A while later at lunch, the animals saw that Toad had returned to his old conceited self. Rat and Badger nodded to Mole and to each other, as if they shared a secret plan.

After lunch, Toad was about to swagger off to write his speeches for the banquet when he suddenly felt himself gripped under each arm by Rat and Badger. They carried him into the library and shut the door.

Dropping him into a chair, Badger stated, "Look here, Toad, we want you to understand that there will be *no* speeches and *no* songs at this banquet. We're not *asking* you; we're *telling* you!"

Toad saw that he was trapped. They saw through him. His dreams of glory for that evening were shattered. "Can't I sing just one little song?" he pleaded.

"No, not one," said Rat firmly. "I know you're disappointed, Toady, but your songs are all

They Carried Him Into the Library.

conceit and boasting, and your speeches are all self-praise and exaggeration and—"

"And full of hot air!" added Badger. "You know we're doing this for your own good, Toad. You simply must turn over a new leaf, and this is the perfect time. Believe me, this hurts all of us more than it hurts you."

Toad sat silently for a while. Then he looked up at his friends and said weakly, "You win. I know you're right and I'm wrong. From now on, I'll be different. You'll never have to be ashamed of me ever again!" Then he pressed his handkerchief to his face and staggered out of the room, sobbing.

"I feel like a brute!" said Rat.

"I know," said Badger. "But it was for his own good. He can't go on being laughed at by stoats and weasels and ferrets, or even by the animals at River Bank."

"I guess we were lucky to have intercepted that little weasel as he was setting out to deliver Toad's invitations. They were simply dis-

He Pressed His Handkerchief to His Face.

graceful! Mole is at Toad's desk this very moment, writing new ones."

By the time Toad reached his bedroom, a sparkle had replaced the tears in his eyes. He locked the door and closed the curtains. Then he placed all the chairs in a semi-circle and stood facing them.

He bowed to his invisible audience, raised his arms, and in a loud, dramatic voice, began to sing a song of praise to Toad on the occasion of his homecoming. The song was cheered wildly by the delighted audience that existed clearly in Toad's imagination!

That evening, Mr. Toad of Toad Hall came down the stairs to greet his guests. All the animals cheered when he entered, crowding around him to congratulate him and praise his courage and his cleverness and his fighting skills.

But Toad only smiled and murmured, "No, no, no! It was Badger who masterminded the whole attack, and it was Mole and Rat who did

His Invisible Audience

most of the fighting. I merely served in the ranks and followed their lead. Really, I did little or nothing at all."

Each time he spoke with such modesty, Toad glanced over at Badger and Rat. They were staring at him with their mouths open in amazement. This gave Toad great satisfaction!

Even when some of the animals called for a speech from him, the master of Toad Hall shook his head modestly and refused, opening his mouth only to say a humble "no."

The banquet was a huge success, and everyone agreed that Toad had indeed changed!

After these events, the four animals continued their lives at River Bank in joy and contentment.

Toad sent a thank-you letter and the gift of a gold locket and chain to the jailer's daughter, and even repaid the barge-woman for the cost of her horse.

On future summer evenings, the friends often took long walks though the Wild Wood,

Toad Had Indeed Changed!

which was now safe and peaceful. Mother weasels even brought their babies to the opening of their holes and pointed out, "See, there goes the great Mr. Toad and the gallant Mr. Rat and the famous Mr. Mole."

But when the little ones misbehaved, their mothers threatened, "The terrible Mr. Badger will come and get you!"

Of course, this was not true at all. Even though Badger didn't much care for society, he *was* rather fond of children. Still, the threat always worked on the mischievous ones . . . and probably still does to this day!